Dear Parent:
Your child's love of reading starts here!

Every child learns to read in a different way and at his or her own speed. Some go back and forth between reading levels and read favorite books again and again. Others read through each level in order. You can help your young reader improve and become more confident by encouraging his or her own interests and abilities. From books your child reads with you to the first books he or she reads alone, there are I Can Read Books for every stage of reading:

SHARED READING
Basic language, word repetition, and whimsical illustrations, ideal for sharing with your emergent reader

BEGINNING READING
Short sentences, familiar words, and simple concepts for children eager to read on their own

READING WITH HELP
Engaging stories, longer sentences, and language play for developing readers

READING ALONE
Complex plots, challenging vocabulary, and high-interest topics for the independent reader

I Can Read Books have introduced children to the joy of reading since 1957. Featuring award-winning authors and illustrators and a fabulous cast of beloved characters, I Can Read Books set the standard for beginning readers.

A lifetime of discovery begins with the magical words **"I Can Read!"**

Visit www.icanread.com for information
on enriching your child's reading experience.

*For young readers around
the world. Never give up.
You can do anything.*
—K.S.L.

For Nate and Marni
—N.M.

I Can Read® and I Can Read Book® are trademarks of HarperCollins Publishers.

Ty's Travels: Zip, Zoom!
Text copyright © 2020 by Kelly Starling Lyons
Illustrations copyright © 2020 by Nina Mata
All rights reserved. Manufactured in U.S.A. No part of this book may be used or reproduced
in any manner whatsoever without written permission except in the case of brief quotations embodied
in critical articles and reviews. For information address HarperCollins Children's Books,
a division of HarperCollins Publishers, 195 Broadway, New York, NY 10007.
www.icanread.com
Library of Congress Control Number: 2019955900
ISBN 978-0-06-295110-6 (trade bdg.)—ISBN 978-0-06-295109-0 (pbk.)

Book design by Rachel Zegar
20 21 22 23 24 LSC 10 9 8 7 6 5 4 3 2
❖
First Edition

I Can Read!

TY'S TRAVELS

Zip, Zoom!

by Kelly Starling Lyons   pictures by Nina Mata

HARPER

An Imprint of HarperCollinsPublishers

I'm Ty.

I have a new scooter.

I can't wait to ride it!

We go to the park.

Daddy and Corey bike.

Momma takes me to scoot.

I put on my knee-pads.

Kids zoom by like race cars.

Vroom, vroom, vroom.

I want to zoom too.

I see the flag waving.

I step on my scooter.

I kick off.

I see crowds watching.
Vroom.

Wobble, wobble.

I do not zip.

I do not zoom.

"Keep going, Ty,"
Momma says.
I think about stopping,
but I do not give up.

11

I see the flag waving.

I step on with one foot.

I kick off with the other.

Cars roar by me.

I focus on the track.

Vroom.

13

Wobble, wobble.

I do not zip.

I do not zoom.

"Almost," Momma says.
I do not give up.

Daddy and Corey ride over.
"You've got this!" Corey says.
"You can do it!" Daddy says.

Momma gives me a thumbs-up.

I see the flag waving.

I step on with one foot.

I push off with the other.

18

My family cheers.

My heart pounds.

I press on the gas.

Vroom, vroom.

Boom.

"Are you OK?" Momma asks.

I sniff and wipe my eyes.

I am on the ground.

That's it!
I GIVE . . .

"Want some help?"
A girl stops her scooter.
She smiles.

"Watch me," she says.

The girl steps on her scooter
with one foot.
She pushes off with the other.
"Hold on," she says.

I see the flag waving.

Look at her go.

27

The girl zooms back to me.
"My name is Ari," she says.

"I'm Ty," I say.

"Ready to try?" Ari asks.

We step on with one foot.

We push off with the other.

We hold on.

I see the flag waving.

Ari zips.

I zoom.

We're racing side by side.

Cameras flash.

Crowds clap.

I didn't give up.

Vroom, vroom, vroom.